COY WOLF

A Langsmith Shifter Short

By Stella Williams

Sequoia Bainbridge reached for the small towel on the hook next to the sink. The rough terry cloth rubbed like sandpaper on her skin, but it was better than letting the arctic winter air dry her face. She smirked at herself in the mirror. A thin golden ring appeared around the deep brown of her almond shaped eyes. Becoming more pronounced the further into shifter territory she got. Even her canines seemed longer and sharper. She pressed one against her full bottom lip and a small drop of blood formed beneath it.

Leaning away from the mirror, Sequoia stretched her arms above her head to loosen some of the tension building in her body. Her wolf would need to run soon. In the meantime, she flexed and fawned over herself in the foggy hotel mirror. In preparation for the annual shifter gathering, Sequoia doubled down on her martial arts training, and it showed. With every move, a delicate ripple of muscle showed beneath her red-brown skin.

The reddish undertone the basis for her name, at least partially. Her mother met her father while on a soul searching trip in Sequoia National Park. According to her mother's oversharing, Sequoia was conceived under the canopy of those large majestic trees. Sequoia's mother always spoke fondly of her father, but Sequoia had no memories of her own. He died before she was born, having been hit by a semi-truck while in wolf form.

"Hurry up, Coy! I've got to pee!"

Sequoia could hear her best friend's dainty feet dancing along the threadbare carpet of their cheap hotel room. Each cotton fiber rasping harshly together almost made Sequoia regret the decision to accept her wolf half. Her mother and paternal grandparents kept the fact that her father was a wolf shifter a secret until her eighteenth birthday. It was rare for a wolf to conceive with a human because most wolves thought mating with a human beneath them.

Sequoia's birthday had fallen on the night of a full moon which totally screwed up her birthday plans. The first signs of her change hit her hard just as she arrived at the dance club with her friends. That's how she met Raya. Sequoia had stumbled away into the nearby alley in the middle of Raya's own transformation. She appeared by Sequoia's side like an angel. Raya's honey-colored skin glistened with the exertion of holding a partial shift. Her wings sprouting from her shoulder blades forming a cocoon around them both. A shield to hide Sequoia while she struggled through the grueling transformation from human to wolf. Raya's eagle guided Sequoia's wolf to a safe place after that change. They became best friends after that.

Sequoia would need a safe place to run again very soon. The closer she got to West Cliff, the harder it became to keep her wolf at bay. Sequoia took one last look at herself before opening the door. Raya ran past her and straight for the toilet. They'd been friends long enough that it didn't bother Sequoia. She needed to get used to it anyway if she wanted to be accepted by the shifter community. They didn't have the same hang-ups as humans when it came to nudity and bodily functions.

"Hurry up, we need to hit the road before the snow starts to fall," Sequoia said slamming the door closed behind her.

"You are so miserly. This is going to be so exciting!"

She ignored her friend's babbling. Sequoia was not usually this brusque, but for what she planned to do, she needed to sharpen her edge. Finding a suitable mate was top on her priority list. In the shifter community that meant maybe a fight or two if her heart decided on a coveted male. Sequoia did not plan to try for an alpha mate at the gathering. Despite her good looks, she was still half human. That disqualified her as a mate for most Alpha males, no matter how high she ranked amongst her peers. Sequoia was also not so keen on throwing herself to the wolves over a man. Something her human half would never reconcile with her wolf half about.

Sequoia checked the time on her phone. Raya would take a while to dress and wouldn't be out of the bathroom again until her makeup was perfect. That gave Sequoia at least an hour to practice.

Living in the city didn't lend to lengthy full moon prowls. It had something to do with vampires and a sort of cold war that was centuries old. Another reason these gatherings were so important. It was just as much about sharing intelligence, as it was challenges and mating.

Raya as a bird shifter had it easy. Their rules for mating were a lot less bound by tradition. Wolf shifters, however, mated based on the notion of survival of the fittest. Alphas had their pick of women, but usually, the strongest of the women were chosen to lead beside them as Alpha female. Status among wolf shifters was everything. That was Sequoia's problem. Her mother had been human, making her weaker than full shifters. Her martial arts training only helped her in human form. Without the last few summers with her grandparents to learn the shifter way of life, her wolf wouldn't stand a chance.

Carefully, she opened the front door. It squeaked on rusty hinges, but not loud enough for Raya to hear over the running shower. Once out of the room, Sequoia took a deep breath to clear the musty smell of the room from her nose. The sun rose over the valley. Devil Wolf Mountain loomed on the horizon casting an ominous shadow. It blocked the rays of sunlight from reaching anything for miles. At least for the next hour or two. Devil Wolf Mountain was her destination. The sight of the annual shifter gathering. It would be her debut as a shifter outside of her father's pack. Her first time actively pursuing a wolf shifter mate.

Sequoia checked her surroundings one last time before slipping into the woods and out of her human skin. With her wolf form completed, her thick black coat kept the winter chill at bay. She allowed her wolf time to prance contentedly through the dry winter forest before pushing her to top speed. She didn't have to be as careful here as she did back home. Wolves were commonplace in this mountain climate. Her wolf ran until she was exhausted before finding a sunny clearing to rest. Now that her wild side was sated, Sequoia could relax into her wolf form. Letting her heightened senses tell her about the world around her. Her wolf licked its chops at the rustling of a fat winter bunny a few feet into the forest. She sniffed the air before beginning to creep forward. Let the hunt begin.

Tyr

Tyr Greywulf reached down to help his sparring partner from his prone position on the ground.

"I don't know why you insist I spar with you. You beat me every time," Otto groaned pulling himself up.

The man stood twice Tyr's size as a bear shifter.

"I need practice with bigger opponents. I won't just be fighting wolves for my spot on top," Tyr replied.

He let go of his friend's hand and snagged the canteen of water from its perch on a fallen log. He took a long drink before offering the container to his longtime friend.

"So you're mate hunting? About time." Otto wiggled a bushy eyebrow at his friend.

Tyr snatched the water away before Otto could bring it to his lips. "Hell, no! I need to cement my alpha status and sew a shit ton more of my wild oats before that ever crosses my mind."

Otto shook his head.
"You never know, maybe the fates will intervene. You know that's been happening more often at these things. God only knows why."

"Nah those matings are anything but fate. There is no such thing. They let a little tail get to their heads is all. That level of possession in unhealthy nothing right or fated about it," Tyr said.

He ran his hand over his head. His fingers running over the coarse black hair that was about half an inch from being a tiny afro. He would need a fresh cut before tomorrow. Even with no plans to search for a mate, he still represented his pack.

"Sure man whatever you say. Be careful out there. You never know when fate might intervene," Otto said with a wink.

The snapping of a nearby twig caught Tyr's attention. His sense went on red alert. Definitely not just passing fauna. He scanned the edge of the clearing and his eyes landed on a black wolf, beyond the first ring of trees surrounding them. In the wolf's mouth hung a fresh kill, rabbit, judging by the size.

Tyr's wolf perked up despite the grueling training he just put it through. Black wolves were rare in the shifter community and even more unique in these parts. Tyr had to focus to keep himself from shifting and greeting the intruder wolf to wolf. It was the first time since puberty he felt unsure of his control over his wolf. As soon as Tyr's made eye contact with the wolf, it lowered its gaze. That angered him, and he didn't know why. As an alpha, he was used to other wolves deferring to him, but somehow this was different.

"Take your kill and go," Tyr snapped, and the wolf did just that.

Tyr followed its movements as it slowly backed away, keeping a wary eye on him and Otto before turning and running.

"I've never seen an all-black wolf before, I wonder if it's some new kid come to take you on," Otto joked.

Tyr scowled at his friend. With the wolf gone, Tyr experienced an inexplicable urge to go after it.

"Me either, but no competitor would submit so easily," Tyr said.

"A spy? I know how competitive you wolf shifters are in your alpha status," Otto said pulling on his coat.

"Maybe," Tyr said.

He didn't believe for a second the black wolf could be a spy. Alpha status among Wolf shifters demanded much more respect than that. It meant you could lead your own pack, have your choice of mate, not to mention the freedom to live by your own rules. No true Alpha would lower themselves to send a spy. Not even against the most feared of competitors. Even those lower in the wolf hierarchy showed more respect than that.

Born to a pair of Omegas, Tyr stood well aware of the limits applied to lower wolves. In the past, Tyr fell way below any ranking shifters' radar. He didn't hate his parents or judge them for their lack of ambition. He needed more out of life than being the comedic relief. He wanted to be the one entertained and exalted. Tyr started challenging his way up the shifter social ladder at the earliest possible age. An excellent strategist and fighter, he only needed a few years of experience under his belt to push him to the top.

Tyr and Otto gathered the rest of their things and headed down the trail to Tyr's truck. The annual gathering started tomorrow and would continue through the weekend. They would need as much rest as possible before the festivities began. The next three days would be filled with mixers and business meetings, but the challenge nights were where Tyr really planned to shine. This year nothing would get in the way of his Alpha goals.

"Oh my god! Can you believe all the hot shifters here? How's a girl to choose," Raya gushed fanning herself.

Sequoia peeked over the event flyer in her hands to see what her friend fussed about. She agreed with her friend. Plenty of fine specimens to ogle around the room, but Sequoia only had eyes for wolf shifters like herself. Raya had a lot more agency with her choice in partner. Wolf shifter females didn't just choose their mates. They fought for them, for the status a mate could provide. Sequoia didn't have any interest in fighting anyone. Not even for the hot shifter she spotted in the woods the day before.

The thought of Mr. Jaw Dropper made Sequoia hot and bothered. She got a pretty good look at him sparring with his bear shifter friend. He stood a little on the short side, but compared to the Huge Bear shifter he fought, almost any man would seem tiny by comparison. She thought of how his ab muscles cut rough planes of burnt sienna before disappearing into his jeans. The image etched into her psyche for life. His full kissable lips made her want to know if they felt as pillow soft against hers as they did in her dreams.

Sequoia pulled a chocolate bar from her purse and took a bite. Not quite the chocolate she was craving at the moment, but it would have to do. She needed to get a grip on her libido if she hoped to achieve her goal for this trip. Today she observed her options. Once she saw where the gorgeous men around her fell in the shifter hierarchy, she would make her choice.

"Easy, stick to the plan," she muttered more to herself than her friend.

Raya smiled brightly at her, undeterred by Sequoia's lack of enthusiasm.

"You know you don't have to stick to wolf shifters. I feel the idea of sticking to one's animal peer is antiquated and a bit incestuous at this stage of the game. You can't tell me that with all the wolves mating each other that there isn't some common link in there somewhere," Raya said.

"All shifters are descended from the same four shifters. Technically we are all family," Sequoia pointed out.

Raya rolled her eyes.

"With an attitude like that, you'll never find the shifter of your dreams," she grumbled.

Sequoia sighed thinking about the shifter that dominated her thoughts since the moment she saw him in the forest. "I don't need the shifter of my dreams. Just one that checks the boxes," Sequoia said.

An eager bunch of shifter women came charging in their direction. Sequoia managed to snag Raya and move out the way before they were trampled. The hair on the back of her neck stood on end.

"Where's the fire," Raya asked.

A chorus of sighs could be heard before either Sequoia or Raya saw what the sent the women in the room into hysteria. Not that Sequoia needed to see for herself. Her body responded the moment he stepped into the room. Mr. Jaw dropper had arrived. His alpha magnetism making all the available shifter women swoon. Sequoia refused to do the same. As a half human, no alpha in their right mind would give her a second glance. Best not even entertain the thought.

"I'm going to go check the challenge roster," Sequoia said.

She didn't bother trying to drag Raya away with her. Raya could throw her hat in that ring if she wanted. That didn't change anything for Sequoia. She found the table set up for challengers to sign up and grabbed the clipboard for female challengers. She might not fight for a man, but she still needed to establish some sort of ranking if she wanted a chance at a suitable mate. Sequoia didn't care much for shifter hierarchy, but her grandparents did. Being an Omega didn't bother her in the least

but having no ranking at all would ruin
her.

Tyr

"Man these things are crazier and crazier, every year." Otto laughed as the crowd of eager women surrounded them.

Tyr shook his head and managed to make enough space to breathe in the chaos. He pushed his way to the front desk to check in. The clerk took his sweet time checking him in. Everyone seemed amused by this debacle but him. So much for keeping his head in the game. On the one hand, it flattered him to know that he had his choice of bed partners. On the other, this year, Tyr needed to avoid any distraction from his goals.

"Hey, man can you check me in too! I can't get through," Otto said.

Tyr peeked back to see his friend being blocked. The gaggle of women turning their flirtations to him. The clerk sped through the usual check-in procedure. At least the man had sense enough to not announce his floor or room number. The clerk slid the key cards in their envelope across the counter, only letting go when Tyr had them both firm in his grasp. The crowd too thick to simply hand the key to Otto, Tyr shoved the keys into his pocket. Otto would have to wait until the novelty wore off and the crowd dispersed.

"Sorry, ladies. I'm not on the market this year," Tyr repeated as he waded through.

His words did nothing to stop their flirting. He looked around for help, but none took the opportunity. All the other men in the room stood awkwardly to the side talking to the few females not tripping over themselves to meet Tyr. Out of the corner of his eye, Tyr spotted a tall, slim figure by the challenge sign up table. His body reacted viscerally even without seeing her face. The little black wolf was a smoking hot female.

Mate. His mind warred with the needs of his body. Courtesy forgotten, Tyr strode right over. The closer he got, the more his wolf urged him forward. He could justify his purposeful stride as an eagerness to register as a challenger, but that would be a blatant lie. He didn't know what about this woman made his wolf go crazy, but his body told him one thing, and one thing only. She belonged to him.

Sequoia

Sequoia stood staring at the list, not reading it, just staring at it. No going back to her human life once she did this. If she didn't put her name on the list. She would be labeled rogue and would be unwelcome in shifter territory. More so than before as a half human shifter.

"Scoping out the competition," a male voice said behind her.

Sequoia whipped around, clutching the clipboard to her chest.

She stared at the massive wall of muscle in front of her, keenly aware of his gaze taking her in. Afraid to meet the eyes of her wolf. She didn't trust herself not to turn into a pile of goo at his feet if she did. Sequoia blinked and shook her head. He didn't belong to her. He could never belong to her. She forced herself not to cower before him and instantly regretted it when her eyes met his. Deep pools of caramel stared back at her, and she clutched the clipboard tighter to keep from reaching up and pulling him down for a kiss.

"Yeah," she breathed.

He flashed his pearly whites before reaching around her body to snag the clipboard for the male challengers. Sequoia hated how her body instinctively leaned closer. Her nostrils flared, catching his earthy masculine scent. Her wolf clawed just beneath the surface. She too couldn't resist the urge to claim the man as hers. He didn't seem to notice her inner turmoil. He casually signed his name in a large swooping scrawl. His signature dominating the line like his body stood dominant to hers.

"Well, I look forward to seeing where you end up," he said.

Mr. Jaw Dropper winked at her before turning and walking away. Her body seemed colder with the absence of his body heat surrounding her. The chill intensified with the realization that everyone stood staring at her. Sequoia turned back to the table and scrawled her name on the paper. It looked rushed and sloppy next to his purposeful artistry. No matter what her body said, Tyr Greywulf, as an alpha, would be nothing but trouble and heartache in the end.

Tyr

Tyr needed some air after that more than casual interaction. His body hummed with sexual tension. His wolf begged to be let out. Tyr waltzed right back out the front doors and shifted into his wolf form. Careful to stay further out from the lodge so he wouldn't come across another shifter prowling. He didn't have to worry about challengers just yet, but his wolf seemed antisocial at the moment. He pushed his wolf to the limit in a vain attempt to drive a certain female from his thoughts.

As a pack leader, Tyr had plenty of other things he could be obsessing over. He alone decided who and what his pack should focus on regarding intelligence gathering. The previous Alpha had been more concerned about petty pack drama than any real work. It was Tyr's job to turn that all around.

In his short time as Pack Leader, he'd already stumbled upon some vital intelligence. The Aura were real and very much still in existence. The group of magic users were the stuff of legend. Most believed their existence a myth, but careful research led to a shocking discovery. Not only were they thriving but had a hidden realm in the middle of his territory.

Magic Users were still a hated group amongst non-humans. He understood that once he reported to the elders, he would need more proof. The word of a teenaged cat shifter wouldn't be sufficient, but for now, that's all he could provide. None of his other assets had managed to get as close as this one little girl. She reminded Tyr of himself at that age. Driven and a little reckless.

On top of the Aura bombshell, there was also the issue of Maura. Yet another supposed myth. The evil vampiress was causing some real damage in his neck of the woods. Drawing too much human attention to the possibility of non-humans in the area. At least he hadn't needed to interfere with that situation yet. The vampires seemed to be handling that one well enough on their own. Tyr ran until the sun sat high in the sky letting him know he needed to wrap things up. He would need some time to get prepared for the first challenges that evening.

Tyr shifted back to human form before entering the clearing where the lodge stood. He could have stayed in wolf form, the gathering had no formal rules about maintaining one form over another. He chose to shift back because he didn't trust his wolf not to go find the woman from earlier. He stopped by the challenge table to take a peek at the challenge roster. He couldn't peruse the female list without arousing suspicion. The table now staffed by two teen shifters, too young to participate in the fun but old enough to be dragged along for the meetings. That didn't stop them from staring and giggling when Tyr got closer.

Not wanting to contribute to any more gossip about himself, he smiled at them and kept moving towards the elevator. The minutes ticked by as the elevator took its time getting back to the lobby. With all the unwanted female attention, Tyr decided it might be best to take the stairs. He just needed to get to his room on the third floor. If he took the stairs at a run, he could count it as further physical training toward his Alpha Goals.

Sequoia

"Oh my god! How lucky are you?"

Raya came rushing over a few minutes after Tyr left. She had been busy cashing in on the attention of all the men the other women in the room had forgotten in Tyr's wake. Apparently, not occupied enough to not make a big deal about the brief moment Sequoia shared with Tyr.

"What? No," Sequoia said.

"Please tell me you are going to at least take that hunk of sex for a test drive,"

Raya gushed.

Sequoia rolled her eyes.

"Uh no, he's an Alpha. I don't have time to play games when I'm on the hunt for a true mate."

Sequoia tried to sound convincing. Either way, neither she nor Raya believed a word she said. She would happily play bedfellows with Tyr if she knew he wouldn't turn tail as soon as he sniffed out her human half. Sequoia left the challenge table and headed for the corridor that would lead to their room. Raya followed, chatting along as if they were safely back at home and not in the midst of shifter drama land.

"Ugh, sweetheart. That's a once in a lifetime chance you're throwing away. Besides, I'm sure not a single guy in here would care if he had a ride first. Hell, it would probably boost their ego to snag the woman who made the Alpha stop and stare," Raya said.

"Yeah until they find out I'm half human," Sequoia said.

They were in the elevator now, headed up to the third floor. Sequoia just needed to make it to her room. Everyone downstairs would hopefully move on from the little scene that played out between her and Tyr. She knew his name now. That made it worse. His name appeared just as sexy as the golden undertones of his flawless complexion. The maker of the universe wasted no inspiration on Tyr Greywulf. His body sculpted to perfection and possessing the charm of a demigod. Tyr could be nothing more than a fantasy to Sequoia.

"Only an asshole who didn't deserve you would care about that anyway. If I were you, I would be more worried about the giant target on your back. Those women were staring daggers at you. Well, me too a little. I'm not perfect. I'm a little jealous but also totes excited for you," Raya continued.

Sequoia leaned against the elevator wall and buried her head in her hands.

"Why is this thing so slow," she groaned.

The elevator stopped. Sequoia charged headfirst out of the door only to run into a brick wall. At least it hurt like a brick wall. Her head began to spin. Someone lifted her from the ground. Now cradled in a pair of strong male arms, Sequoia seemed enveloped in an achingly familiar scent.

"You, what room is she in," Tyr's voice reverberated through her body.

Arousal pooled between her legs at the sound. She registered a new stiffness in his body. Tyr's wolf senses having picked up on her body's stupidity in this close proximity or maybe the fact she was half human. At least she didn't have to dwell on it long. Raya responding to his alpha command moved quickly to do his bidding. He carried Sequoia to her hotel room and placed her on the bed. She didn't even have time to thank him before he rushed out.

With him gone, she experienced a deep sense of longing. Her wolf moping at the loss of what she deemed her mate. Sequoia waited a moment before opening her eyes again. Raya stared right at her with a knowing smile.

"Don't look at me like that," Sequoia snapped.

Tyr represented everything she didn't want or need. No matter what her nosy friend and stubborn wolf seemed to think.

Tyr leaned against the wall while waiting for the elevator to come back up. It took every ounce of discipline to keep himself from going back into her room.

"Look, man. I know you are dead set on making a name for yourself, but a hot piece of ass like that? She's not going to stay on the market long," Otto said.

Tyr shot his friend a dirty look. "Don't call her a piece of ass," he ground out.

"Sorry man didn't mean to offend." Otto put his hands up in a mock defensive gesture.

"If you say sorry to anyone it should be her! You should have moved out of her way," Tyr snapped.

His wolf paced in anger, just as pissed as Tyr. No one talked about his woman that way. Any male shifter worth his salt understood not to mess with another's mate. *Mate,* the word sounded in Tyr's head like the clang of a warning bell. His agenda didn't allow for mate hunting. As much as he would love to spend the weekend getting physical with the female, his bid for Alpha came first.

"Right, I'll tell her when I see her later," Otto said.

"You're seeing her later?"

Tyr's wolf threatened to come out and tear out Otto's throat. No matter how much his body lusted after the woman, he needed his wolf back in line. Tyr needed to get back in control if he had any chance of defending and advancing his status as an Alpha. Besides wolf females didn't go for other shifters, at least most of them didn't. Something told Tyr, Sequoia might be an exception to that rule. She did hang out with a bird shifter. The thought was like a hot poker to his heart.

"Not her. While you were getting all caveman over your mate, I made plans with her hot little friend," Otto said with a wag of his eyebrows.

The ding of the elevator arriving cut their conversation short. A gaggle of wide-eyed beauties stared back at the two shifters. Tyr would have headed back to his room if he didn't need to go back down to the lobby for the first meeting of the afternoon. As pack leader, it was his job to inform the elders of relevant information gathered by his pack. Shifters survived on knowing everyone's secrets and trading that information when advantageous.

Humans weren't the only threat in the world. Vampires and Magic users needed to be kept tabs on as well. If any of their secrets fell into the wrong hands, it could be the end to all non-humans. Otto got into the elevator first, making small talk with the women. In no mood for all of their fawning, Tyr decided not to follow.

"I think I'll take the stairs," he said and took off before any of the women could attempt to convince him to ride with them.

Back home, Tyr had a solid reputation with the ladies but nothing compared to the sheer intensity of a couple hundred man-hungry female shifters. When he first arrived, it took real strength of will to keep himself from bolting right back out the door. He thought all that temptation would dissipate once more shifters had come. Entering the lobby, he realized his lack of insight. Bombarded by women, he put on the charm. Only this time the women held no interest to him. Not because he kept his head in the game. Far from it. His wolf had its heart set on Sequoia and Tyr learned from experience that his wolf could be a stubborn SOB.

Sequoia

Sequoia fussed with the drawstring of her sweats for the fifteenth time since she arrived in the challenge arena. The women's challenges were about to begin. Sequoia fought the urge to pace, more than a little nervous. Only wolf shifter women participated in challenges. They happened deep in the woods far from the crowds of the gathering. Not that anyone really cared to watch the women like they did the men.

"You sure you want to do this?"

Raya glanced around the clearing at the various women. All wolf shifters, and all of them shooting daggers in Sequoias direction.

"I don't have a choice. I'll be fine. Just a few wrestling matches to prove I'm not weak and then I can bow out gracefully to join the party tonight."

Her plan had been foolproof until Tyr. Sequoia would need to fight harder than she imagined to save face. These women were pissed and out for blood. There were unspoken rules about not doing any lasting damage to each other. No shots to the face or arms. No intentional bruising if possible. Challenges were about establishing dominance without ruining each other's chance of finding a mate. No man wanted a bruised and battered woman.

"Sequoia Bainbridge and Elena Lupus!"

The elder alpha female called from the center of the clearing. Time for Sequoia's first round. She squeezed her hands into fists at her side to keep everyone from seeing how they tremored. Sequoia had trained all year for this very moment. That didn't stop her from being terrified. This one moment would define how respected she became amongst the shifter community. She would either win their acceptance or further cement the idea that she, as a half shifter, didn't belong.

She met her opponent at the center of the ring. She extended her hand for the woman to shake. A sign of good sportsmanship, or so Sequoia thought. The woman took her hand and squeezed with all her might.

Elena's eyes danced with fire as she leaned in closer to Sequoia. "After I beat you, you will stay away from Tyr."

So much for a friendly fight. Elena had it out for her because of one brief encounter with Tyr. Sequoia squeezed the woman's hand back and tried not to enjoy the slight wince she made.

"After I beat you, you are welcome to him."

Sequoia said the words but didn't mean them. Tyr dominated her thoughts since their first encounter in the woods. Her wolf already decided. She wanted him as her mate. There was no denying that, but that didn't mean Sequoia was willing to fight the hundreds of women who also wanted him. She would stick to her plan, but first, she would put Ms. Lupus in her place.

Tyr

Thwack. Tyr's fist connected with his opponent's face. *Thud.* The challenger fell to the ground before he even had a chance to break a sweat. One punch and the man was on his back. Tyr stalked toward the man who quickly scrambled to his knees and bowed before him. Keeping his head and gaze lowered.

"I recognize your superior might and graciously forfeit," the words so soft and rushed that Tyr almost didn't hear them.

It was a shame, the lack of ambition. If the man couldn't handle a single punch, he was destined for Omega status. Why

Tyr had been paired with someone so far below his ability was a mystery.

"Go," he spat at his opponent.

The man stood and quickly shuffled away while Gary the elder assigned as tonight's witness strode into the makeshift ring shaking his head. In the past, even the weakest Omega lasted a few rounds. It seemed a new breed of shifter had cropped up in the last few years. Before Tyr stepped into the ring, three other challenges were decided in their first round.

"Tyr Greywulf has once again proven his ability," Gary announced.

It gave Tyr no joy or sense of accomplishment even as the bloodthirsty crowd cheered his victory. Gary didn't raise Tyr's hand as the victor. He too understood the match had been poorly selected. All of the matches that evening had been. Either someone screwed up, or it was a deliberate attempt to weed out the weak-willed from the very start.

Tyr was one step closer to the alpha status he craved but not like this. He wanted to earn it the right way. There was no honor in pummeling the defenseless. Angrily, Tyr stormed out of the ring. The crowd parting for him without being asked. His vibe was not very welcoming at the moment. The freedom of the forest beckoned him. A place where he could release his unsportsmanlike frustrations. Instead, he headed inside to the nightly gathering.

Women dressed in scraps of fabric meant to lure and captivate male attention lined the walls. The men freshly showered and some even shaved, mingled and discussed business. It was all very archaic, but there was something to be said for tradition in this case. Shifters could pretend to be normal humans all they liked, but in the end, they were part animal. Base instinct often overruled intelligent thought. Male dominance was part and parcel of the mating equation even for the freest thinking shifters.

Several women attempted to catch Tyr's eye. He didn't pay them any mind. His only goal, to be present enough to appease the masses before making a getaway to the solitude of his room. He had to keep his wits about him for his next challenge. That meant avoiding any situation that put him within range of Sequoia. The little black wolf would be his undoing.

Sequoia

Exhausted and sweaty, Sequoia took the stairs two at a time up to her room. She thought it best to avoid the crowded elevator after what happened earlier. The embarrassment of the moment killed her euphoric victory buzz. Elena Lupus turned out to be all talk and no fight. Sequoia hardly laid a finger on her before the poor thing cowered away.

That being said the next four women who signed up to challenge her that day were much tougher opponents. Sequoia loved grappling, but her weekly jujitsu class never worked her over this hard. Her entire body ached. Covered in dirt from head to toe, Sequoia wanted to take a hot shower and crawl into bed for the night. Unfortunately, Sequoia already promised Raya that she wouldn't take long getting ready and join her at the already raging party.

Sequoia pushed open the door to her floor and stopped in her tracks. None other than Tyr came out of the elevator at that precise moment. For a second she contemplated ducking back into the stairwell, but her wolf made her stay put. She saw the tension in his body shift as his gaze fell on her. She watched helplessly as he took long strides down the hall toward her.

"Who did this to you?"

He took her chin in his hand and studied her face. Sequoia caught a few errant blows during her challenges that left some minor bruises. Nothing that would warrant such scrutiny. She took a reluctant step back and out of his grip.

"I'm fine," she said. Sequoia tried to move passed his massive body, but he was quicker than she was.

"You are not fine! You're bleeding," Tyr said.

She saw him looking in the area of her eyebrow and reached up to touch the tender spot on her face. Sure enough, her fingers were red with blood. Not a lot but enough to elicit Tyr's anger and make her feel a little woozy. She had never done well with blood. Tyr's arms were around her once again, and this time he guided her to his room. He made her sit while he fished out a first aid kit and set to work cleaning and tending to her wound.

"You don't have to do this. I can handle it myself," she snapped.

He shook his head and continued what he was doing. "You must have really pissed someone off for them to mar your face in a challenge."

Being this close to him, it was hard to keep her reckless emotions at bay. Especially with how he looked at her when he didn't think she was paying him attention.

"My only crime was having the misfortune of getting too close to you. Not all of us have the alpha charisma to make it through challenges relatively unharmed." She tried to divert the attention from herself.

She was becoming self-conscious under his intense scrutiny. It was obvious he wanted her too, and that was the sucky part. If she gave in, there would be hell to pay. Not just in the challenge ring, but in her outside life as well. Once she had an idea of what being with an alpha was like,

she wouldn't be able to resign herself to
being with anyone else. She wouldn't even
begin to fool herself into thinking Tyr
would want more than just one night with
her.

Tyr

Tyr stopped what he was doing and looked her dead in the eyes. She averted her gaze out of habit, bowing her head in deference even as her wolf protested. She may have come out of the ring a little worse for wear, but at the moment, she was on an equal footing with him. An alpha because just like in her human life she couldn't let the bullies win.

"If you think my charm had anything to do with me being an Alpha, you are sadly mistaken. You are just as much alpha as I am. I knew it the moment I saw you spying on me in the woods. You just need to act like it," Tyr said gruffly and stood.

"How did you know it was me?" She focused on the floor not him.

Tyr was used to that from others. He didn't want that from her. "I didn't, but my wolf recognized you the moment we met at the challenge table."

Tyr pulled her into his arms and forced her to meet his gaze.

"Really?" she said, just above a whisper.

Tyr and his wolf were confounded by this woman. They both recognized her alpha status and yet she kept forcing herself into a submissive role. In any other wolf, he allowed it but not her. Not his mate. One way or another he would show her that she didn't need to hide who she was. Not from anyone and surely not from him.

"You want to know what else it recognized about you."

A cocky grin spread across his face.

"What?"

He loved how breathless she seemed around him. It was the only sign of their shared attraction she allowed.
He leaned closer to whisper in her ear, "How about I show you instead?"

His lips brushed across her earlobe ever so slightly, and she shivered against him. This was it. This was the moment that they both seemed to be avoiding. There would be no hiding what his mind screamed every time she was near. If she allowed him to continue on this dangerous path. It was now or never.

"Yes!"

The words had barely left her mouth
before he lost control. He claimed her lips,
not minding the salty, earthy flavor of the
dust and grime that still covered her. Their
lips melded together, and Sequoia relaxed
into his embrace. The feel of her surrender
was so sweet, he nearly stopped to savor
the moment. At least until her hands
wrapped around his neck and urged him to
continue. Tyr pushed her back onto the
bed. He would have her tonight but not
wholly. That would have to wait until he
was sure she would welcome his claim on
her. Not just as a bedfellow but as a mate.

Sequoia

She'd lost her mind. Sequoia was sure of it, but that didn't stop her from enjoying her taste of forbidden fruit. Tyr didn't seem to mind that she was covered in dust and sweat as he stared down at her naked body. His eyes gleaming with pleasure and indecision. He licked his full lips as he perused what she had to offer.

"Like what you see?"

Sequoia knew the answer to that question, but she wanted to hear him say it. Needed that bit of reassurance as she laid herself bare before him. Tyr smiled and ran a hand along her thigh before taking hold of her ankles and pulling her closer to the edge of the bed.

"I do," he said before taking her mouth once again.

Sequoia was no virgin, but he made her feel like it was her first time. No man had ever looked at her the way he did. Hell, most didn't bother to keep the lights on longer than it took to get them both naked. Let alone spend several agonizing minutes devouring her body with their eyes. It was as if he silently acknowledged that this would be their first and last time together. Wanted to memorize every minute of it. Sequoia tried not to dwell on that as he trailed kisses down her neck.

His rough hands gliding against her wet folds. She gasped when he slid one thick finger into her and then two. It was silly really. Her body reacted like an eager hormonal teenager. His every touch sent electricity dancing across her nerve endings. Slow, measured movements building the tension in her body before Tyr intentionally switched tactics. Thumb pressed firmly against her clit, while his index finger swirled around her entrance. Just barely sliding into her leaving her hanging on the precipice, desperate to jump.

"Please," she begged as he slid his hand from her body a fourth time.

She watched as he sucked her juices from his fingers. A low rumble of pleasure came from his throat.

"My pleasure," he growled and slid off the bed.

Sequoia started to sit up, but he tugged at her ankles again. This time bringing them around his neck before his wicked tongue laved her lower lips.

"Oh my," Sequoia cried as he licked and suckled her into oblivion.

She thought he would stop once the last waves of her orgasm subsided, but he had other ideas. She felt him grin against her before she was suddenly flipped onto her stomach. She felt the urge to crawl away as soon as his hot breath tickled her exposed cheeks, but he held her in place. Hands anchored on her hips, pulling her closer to his magic tongue. Her hands gripped the sheets tightly as he continued his oral onslaught this time on the pucker of her asshole. No one had ever done that to her before. She never thought it was something she would ever have enjoyed, but Tyr was proving her wrong on that front.

Not to be outdone, Sequoia walked her hands across the bed until her face was positioned in range of his turgid flesh. Now with him so close she hesitated. His girth and length were even more impressive up close. She licked her lips before flicking her tongue out to tease the tip of him. Tyr hissed and pressed his hips forward. It was safe to say he wouldn't protest a little mutual gratification. She left him hanging for a moment. The soft skin like silk dancing across her lips.

Tyr hefted her up higher onto his shoulders and knelt on the edge of the bed. Sequoia gasped at the movement, his manhood sliding past parted lips. She smiled before relaxing her jaw to take him in completely. Tyr's groan of appreciation vibrated against her sensitive flesh. If he kept it up, she wouldn't last much longer.

Sequoia wanted to make him come before he had a chance to make her a second time. She worked him as best as she could in her inverted position. She took her cues from him, suckling until he was moaning into her. She let him slide from her mouth before teasing the tip of him with her tongue and teeth. His hips rocked back and forth, urging her to continue. He grew incredibly hard. The firm length pressing deeper into her mouth with each thrust of his hips. Then suddenly, he stilled, holding himself as far as she allowed. He released a mighty roar. Warm salty jets spilled down her throat.

Sequoia saw stars as a second orgasm screamed through her. He fell from her mouth as she screamed her pleasure around him. Tyr patiently continued until it faded before letting her jellied limbs fall to the mattress.

"Stay," he barked before disappearing to the bathroom.

Sequoia smiled to herself. She couldn't have moved if she wanted to. Her whole body abuzz with post-orgasmic bliss. Even her wolf was content to stay put. Both females excited for what could happen next. At least for tonight.

Tyr did his best not to let his ego be bruised by the fact Sequoia was gone when he woke up. The sheets still warm from her body heat, it was the door softly closing that had woken him. He sighed. Staring up at the ceiling, Tyr pondered the fantastic night they spent together.

His dick tented in the sheets at the thought. Sequoia was perfect. Tyr typically rushed through oral sex, but with her, he never wanted to stop. She tasted of pine and honey, and her mouth on him had seemed like heaven. He couldn't wait to get her back into his bed later. As soon as he was done with the night's challenges he would track her down and make her his for good.

A loud knock on the door stole the last moments of frivolity from him. He peeked over at the clock and cursed. He was way behind schedule which meant the rude intrusion was probably Otto coming to get him. Tyr rolled out of bed and grabbed the sweats he discarded last night. Otto was leaning against the wall with a knowing smirk on his face when Tyr opened the door.

"Long night?" Otto laughed.

Normally, Tyr wouldn't hesitate to kiss and tell with his best friend but not about Sequoia.

"I didn't miss anything big, did I?"

Otto shook his head before handing Tyr the latest challenge roster. Tyr had fallen to fifth place in his absence. That made his stomach sink. He didn't regret one minute of his time with Sequoia, but he couldn't abide the current outcome. If the fates had allowed him to avoid her as planned, he wouldn't have fallen so far behind. Once again, proving that his attraction to her was something he needed to keep under wraps for a bit longer. Last night had only made it harder for him to do so.

"Shit, I better get down there," Tyr said.

Otto nodded and followed him to the elevator. Tyr didn't even stop to grab something to eat. He just headed straight for the challenge ring. He had too much ground to cover at this point to focus on anything but. At least until he saw Sequoia in the lobby. Sequoia wore a pair of black leggings and an oversized sweater that hung from one shoulder. Her clothing exposing far too much of her mahogany skin for his liking.

Her thick black curls framed her face in delicate spirals and drew your eyes to her ruby stained lips. To make matters worse, she was holding court with three shifter males, smiling and laughing almost effortlessly. Tyr recognized Otto's hand on his shoulder before he registered that he changed direction. Without intervention, he would have charged right into the group.

"Good Morning, Sequoia!" Otto said.

"Hi, Otto," Sequoia said pleasantly enough, but her eyes cut daggers at Tyr.

"Sorry to barge over like this. I was wondering if you could tell me where Raya is," Otto continued after another awkward moment of Tyr and Sequoia just staring at each other.

Tyr would have thanked Otto for his attempt to justify their presence there, but it didn't matter. It was apparent to the lesser shifters that Tyr had other motives than to make pleasantries. Sequoia broke eye contact first, leaving Tyr feeling like even more of an ass.

"She had a long night. I'm sure she will be down shortly," Sequoia said to Otto.

They continued to chat for a moment. Tyr didn't pay attention to a word that was being said. He hated feeling so off-kilter. Tyr forced himself to look away from her. She had a right to explore her options. Maybe what he felt between them was only one-sided. Tyr excused himself and continued his path to the ring. He was pissed, and the Challenges were the perfect place to vent his frustrations.

Sequoia

Otto was a good friend, but Sequoia was pissed that he seemed adamant to hold her attention all day. Even after Raya came down from her room, he stuck by her side, making ordinary conversation and keeping all other suitors at bay. She was upset, but also a little grateful for the interference. Her rank had fallen significantly since last night, but Sequoia didn't mind. Being a beta was something she was more than happy to live with. Still, her goal had been to find a mate and Otto was impeding her progress.

Tomorrow was the last day of the event. That meant tonight was key in securing someone worthy of her time. Someone who checked her boxes and proved themselves decent in bed. Sequoia may be willing to sacrifice fairytale romance in finding a mate, but not good sex. Sequoia couldn't be sure anyone would ever stack up to the insane pleasure she shared with Tyr. Forgetting about him wasn't going to be easy, but it was a necessity.

She wanted to avoid any more time in the challenge ring. Sequoia didn't have to worry about Elena any longer. There were plenty of others who would literally kill for a chance to be with Tyr. Knowing what she did now, she honestly couldn't blame them.

With Otto permanently attached to her side, Sequoia decided she could at least be nice and go watch the challenges. The male challenges were too violent for her liking, but part of her was interested in seeing Tyr in his element. Once at the ring, Otto got lost in the energy of the crowd. Her bodyguard distracted, he missed the opportunity to interfere when a surprising new suitor sidled up to her.

"Micco Dinali," he introduced himself.

"Sequoia," she said purposefully leaving off her last name.

Rule one of courting was not to give one's full name to just any shifter. Wolf shifters were very territorial. If they got it in their heads that you were theirs, they were known to track a woman down and make it so. Sequoia didn't want it to be that easy for a spurned suitor to find her.

"I noticed your ranking. You don't strike me as the quitting type," Micco said.

Sequoia scowled at him.

"It's not quitting. It's a conscious choice. I don't believe any man is worth risking life or limb over," she replied.

"Until you met me." He smiled.

Micco was obviously full of himself, and he was beginning to annoy her. She was just about to tell him off when she spotted Tyr across the room glaring at them. They made eye contact, and Sequoia suddenly felt guilty for even entertaining the possibility of a different suitor. She didn't like the feeling not one bit, but she also wouldn't be sucked in that easy. As amazing as last night had been, he held back from her. Their interaction hot but limited, and Sequoia could only guess as to why.

She didn't want game playing Alphas. She wanted an uncomplicated partnership. Roaring fires died out quicker than smoldering coals. So she pasted on a smile and giggled like Micco had said the most hilarious thing.

Micco seemed pleased by her attention despite the fact she was not into what he was offering. At least she didn't have to suffer him long. The elder stepped into the ring and called the next challengers.

"Micco Dinali and Tyr Greywulf!"

Tyr circled his opponent, studying the man from head to toe. He was taller than Tyr by a good foot in height. His dark skin the color of burnt wood with a blue undertone that made him look as if he could blend seamlessly with the night sky. It made Tyr think of Sequoia's wolf.

Just as black and alluring. Micco and Sequoia would make a striking pair if that were her choice. The thought rubbed Tyr the wrong way, but it was clear he was just one in a sea of willing suitors. His alpha status in no way helped him in winning her heart.

She was so different from the other female wolves he knew. Not just in personality. There was something about her that he just couldn't quite place. Tyr's moment of distraction cost him dearly. While he was pondering Sequoia, his opponent had moved into Tyr's personal sphere. Landing a blow right across his jaw and sending Tyr sprawling backward.

He was able to catch himself before he hit the ground, throwing his body forward he swung wildly in an attempt to counter the attack. It forced the other wolf to take a step back, giving Tyr the space he needed to get himself together. Even with his mind not entirely in the right place.

Tyr glared at his opponent. He couldn't afford to be caught off guard again. This fight was his to lose. They both knew it. Not just in the ring but with Sequoia. A fact only cemented by her movement toward the door. She was giving up on him before the fight had even begun and Tyr wasn't going to take that lying down.

The two men circled each other, once, twice, a third time. Neither one of them wanting to risk a move without calculating the outcomes. Tyr had to give it to the guy. He may not be a heavy hitter like Tyr, but he was smart and calculating. That gave Tyr his motivation to strike. He would overpower the man with his physical strength. You couldn't come up with a solid attack plan if there were no time to come off the defensive.

With his plan set, Tyr lunged for the man. Not settling for simple jabs but going straight for the grapple. He took out his legs, grounding Micco before twisting his long limbs into a nice little pretzel. It all happened before the guy could blink twice. Tyr had him in an armbar, but the wolf in him made him reposition into a rear naked choke. Nothing satisfied his animal instinct like going for the throat.

Micco put up a good fight. He landed a few weak blows with one hand while trying to relieve the pressure on his neck with the other. It didn't matter. Tyr knew he was the stronger man and Micco's movements were getting sluggish. He had to give Micco credit for not immediately tapping out but as competitive as Tyr was he didn't want to actually hurt the man.

The elder in charge stepped in to call the fight. Tyr was the victor. Micco had been his last challenger. He'd achieved his goal of being the ultimate Alpha. So why did he still feel empty inside? His wolf knew the answer. He could be the baddest wolf in the world, and it wouldn't matter because he wasn't with the baddest female, Sequoia.

Sequoia

Sequoia adjusted the loose shoulder of her sweater and forced a smile at the man before her. Despite her efforts to change the topic of conversation, he insisted on regaling her of all the things he felt a proper mate should be. None of them fit her at all, but there was no way of politely extricating herself from the conversation.

With Raya keeping tabs on the challenge roster for Sequoia, she didn't have her there as an easy out either. Otherwise, Raya would be right there next to her and Otto. Raya and Otto were somehow a thing. The budding romance kept Raya distracted, leaving Sequoia to check out her sliming options for a mate alone.

"You're almost Omega status now. Are you sure you don't want to jump in there one last time?" Raya cut in sidling up to Otto and Sequoia.

Sequoia smiled at her friend and nodded. "You're right. I should be a little more ambitious than this." Sequoia handed her drink to the man and walked away without a word more.

If that were the kind of guy being an Omega would afford her, she needed to adjust her plans. Finding the challenge roster, she picked the top female and put her name next to it. She didn't have to win the fight against Luna Lupine, just last through to a second round. Her status would then be bolstered to something more tolerable to a higher ranked male.

That was the new plan. At least until Sequoia stepped into the ring. The Amazon of a woman before her smirked at Sequoia's willowy frame. The woman made a show of flexing her muscles, perfectly highlighted by the overly spray tanned skin. She looked more bench press Barbie than Catfight Cindy, but Sequoia would show her.

"I hope you aren't challenging me just for a chance with Tyr. An alpha like him won't stand a bastard half breed no matter how high your ranking," Luna spat.

Sequoia bristled. She may not be willing to fight dirty over a man, but no one called her names without repercussion. She didn't bother with providing an oral response. Her swift sweep of the woman's legs was answer enough.

Luna landed with a hard thud, the ground shaking under the impact. Anger flashed in her eyes and Sequoia realized if she let the woman have another second of air there would be hell to play. Sequoia knew precisely what to do. She needed to use her secret weapon. A fail-safe in case the challenges proved more intense than she anticipated. With three precise strikes, Sequoia temporarily paralyzed her opponent.

The women around her all gasped in horror as Sequoia stood over what had once been the top Alpha female. Whispers of cheating floated through the crowd. Sequoia didn't stay long enough for the elder female to call the match. She walked right out the ring and headed straight for her room. This was not how she planned for things to be. She only wanted to gain a little respect, and now she'd ruined everything.

Tyr

Tyr's search for Sequoia didn't last long. Otto waited for him at the entrance to the challenge ring a grim set to his face.

"Sequoia's in trouble," Otto said.

"What? How?"

"Better if you see for yourself," he said.

Tyr followed his friend from the challenge ring and toward the crowd of people hanging by the main meeting room. Between Otto's massive size and Tyr's anxious vibe, the sea of shifters parted like the red sea. Tyr nearly tripped over the giant woman laying eyes wide open on a stretcher on the floor. Sequoia stood before the council of elders with her head hung low. He didn't care what it looked like. She was his mate, and he was going to stand by her. No matter what was happening here. She looked over at him when he reached her. He took her hand in his and squared off with the elders.

"What are the charges?" he demanded.

"Tyr don't. It's all just a misunderstanding," Sequoia said.

She attempted to pull her hand from his grasp.

"Sequoia Bainbridge, half wolf clan half human. You are charged with the unlawful use of magic in a challenge,"

Gary said.

"Magic? Half wolf clan?" Tyr was having a hard time fitting the pieces together.

"It's not magic. I told you it's pressure points. Any idiot can look it up online. It takes practice to learn how to do it correctly and without permanent damage," Sequoia said, still not looking up.

Tyr grabbed her shoulders and made her look into his eyes. Having experienced Aura energy for himself, Tyr was certain she hadn't used any magic. Yet, she didn't deny the claim that she was half human. It didn't matter to him personally. What mattered was that she was in trouble and only minimally defending herself.

"Show me how to do it. I will prove it isn't magic," he said.

"I can't risk it. It's an exact maneuver," Sequoia said.

Tyr shook his head.

"Trust in me, my mate," he said.

Her lips parted in surprise. Tyr couldn't help but lean in to kiss her. They got swept up in each other until one of the elders cleared their throat.

"Even if I could teach you, who would volunteer to be your guinea pig? I'd say you could use it on me, but then I couldn't undo it once it was done," she said.

Tyr frowned. She was right. He'd seen something similar in his martial arts research. It was something a lot more complicated than it looked. He looked around the room and waved Otto over.

"Otto, would you mind?" he asked.

Otto shook his head. "Whatever, man as long as I don't end up a vegetable. You aren't the only one with a new mate to claim," he grumbled before flashing a grin at Raya who was blushing profusely.

Tyr paid close attention to Sequoia's instructions. Soon Otto was prone on his back in the same state as the female. Sequoia then undid what they had just done and did the same to the female.

"See not magic. Just technique," Sequoia said.

Tyr pulled Sequoia into his arms as the elders huddled to decide her fate.

"You didn't have to do this," she said.

"Of course I did. What kind of Mate would I be if I didn't do everything in my power to protect my female," he said.

She bit her lip before leaning in and kissing him. "Your female?"

"Damn straight. From the moment I laid eyes on you," Tyr said.

"I guess I can live with that," she teased.

Tyr pulled back a little. "You guess?"

"Well, you haven't shown me what all I'd be committing to," Sequoia said.

"Oh I will, as soon as we are done here," Tyr promised.

His body was already eager to see to the task, but it would have to wait for the elders' judgment. Thankfully, they didn't have to wait long.

"Sequoia Bainbridge, you are cleared of all charges and released to your mate. Keep an eye on her Tyr," Gary said with a slight smile.

"You bet I will," Tyr said.

He lifted Sequoia off her feet and tossed her over his shoulder. Now that he had his forever mate, he wouldn't let her get cold feet before he could stake his claim once and for all.

THE END

About the Author

Stella Williams is a Blogger and Romance Author, who lives in Washington State. She has a degree in Anthropology from The University of California, Santa Cruz.

Keep Up to date with Stella Williams

Website
www.serpentinecreative.com

Facebook Fan Page
www.facebook.com/stellawilliamsaut
hor

Mailing List
https://mailchi.mp/2637cc1d4d12/get
creative

Instagram
www.instagram.com/stellalove4life

YouTube
http://www.youtube.com/c/SerpentineCreative

Twitter
www.twitter.com/stellalove4life

Stella's Catalogue

<u>Maura's Men Trilogy</u>

Xander's Claim
https://amzn.to/2P79iZ1

Claude's Conquest
https://amzn.to/2PaZlKe

Shane's Redemption
https://amzn.to/2yHkeXt

Maura's Men Complete
Trilogy
https://amzn.to/31HP534

<u>**Secret of Ceres**</u>

Ferocious
https://amzn.to/2CKhKcg

<u>**Langsmith Shifters**</u>

Coy Wolf